ond upon Thames Libraries

www.richmond.gov.uk/libraries

LONDON BOROUGH OF
RICHMOND UPON THAMES

To my grandchildren with all my love.
Be brave, be yourselves and try to be
the best 'you' you can be!

Quarto is the authority on a wide range of topics.

Quarto educates, entertains and enriches the lives of our readers—enthusiasts and lovers of hands-on living.

www.quartoknows.com

Written and illustrated by Steve Smallman

This edition first published in 2021 by Happy Yak,
an imprint of The Quarto Group.
The Old Brewery, 6 Blundell Street,
London N7 9BH, United Kingdom.
T (0)20 7700 6700 F (0)20 7700 8066
www.QuartoKnows.com

A catalogue record for this book is available from the British Library.

ISBN 978 0 7112 5881 5

Manufactured in Guangzhou, China EB042021

9 8 7 6 5 4 3 2 1

MIX
Paper from
responsible sources
FSC
www.fsc.org
FSC® C124385

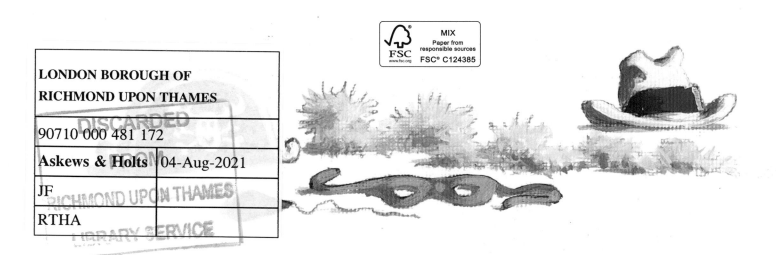

The MOOSE FAIRY

STEVE SMALLMAN

happy yak

Moose was walking through the forest one day when he saw a poster.

❋ Secret Fairy Club ❋

NEW MEMBERS WANTED!

Meeting today, 11 o'clock
at the Old Oak Tree.

❋Bring your own costume.❋
❋ Free fairy cakes! ❋
❋All welcome!❋

P.S. TOP SECRET.

Moose couldn't believe his luck.
He had always wanted to be a fairy!

"I must find something to wear!" he
thought, and he ran off to get ready.

Back at home, Moose looked through his dressing-up box and tried on some outfits.

Could this work? No.

A clown fairy? No.

This hat? No.

Aha, my wand
and crown!

TA-DA...
this is the one!

Moose felt fabulous in his fairy costume. But when he arrived at the Old Oak Tree, he couldn't help but notice that everybody else was... well, little!

"What are *you* doing here?" asked Mouse, rudely.

"I've come to join the Secret Fairy Club," replied Moose, in a loud whisper.

"**Shhhhh!**" said the others,
"It's a secret!"

"But the poster said *All Welcome*,"
replied Moose, confused.

"You are welcome, Moose,"
said Miss Twinkle, the head fairy.
"Now, time for the tests, everyone!"

There was a twirling test,

a wand waving test,

and a making-glitter-pictures test.
Moose loved them all!

Then they had to
say the fairy oath.

"Fairies are kind to all creatures,
Fairies are not mean or bitter,
Fairies help others in trouble or need,
And make pretty pictures with glitter!"

"Well done, everyone!" said
Miss Twinkle, "you've all passed!"

Moose was so excited!

Next, Miss Twinkle taught them the secret knock to open the clubhouse door.

"Why don't you try it first, Moose?" she said.

KNOCK KNOCK,
KNOCKITY KNOCK,
KNOCK,
KNOCK,
KNOCK!

As if by magic,
the secret door opened.

But it was tiny!

Everybody else ran, laughing, into the clubhouse... but poor Moose was left outside.

The rude little Mouse stuck her head out of a window. "You can't be in our club," she said. "You just don't fit in!"

Feeling miserable, Moose walked away.

"Having a bath, Moose?" asked Fox,
as he watched from the riverbank.

"No," sighed Moose, "I'm trying to shrink so
I can get into the Secret Fairy Club and
eat fairy cakes with all the little creatures."

Fox thought of all those little
creatures stuffed with fairy
cakes. "Sounds delicious!"
he grinned.

"I think I'd like
to join, too."

"It's in the Old Oak Tree," said Moose, miserably.
"The secret knock goes *knock knock, knockity knock,
knock, knock, knock.* But don't tell anyone. It's a secret."

But Fox had already gone.

Back in the Old Oak Tree, Miss Twinkle looked around. "Where's Moose?" she asked. The fairies looked at each other, rather sheepishly.

"He's gone!" wailed Beaver.

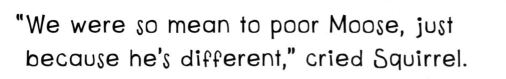

"We were so mean to poor Moose, just because he's different," cried Squirrel.

"He was brilliant at glitter pictures," said Mouse, quietly.

Just then... KNOCK KNOCK, KNOCKITY KNOCK, KNOCK, KNOCK, KNOCK!

"Moose!" they cheered.
"You're just in time for..."

"DINNER!" growled Fox, squeezing through the door.

Meanwhile, Moose, dripping with water, approached the Old Oak Tree. "Maybe I've shrunk by now," he thought.

Suddenly Moose heard a cry.

"HEEEEEEEELP!"

He rushed to the tree...
but couldn't get inside!

"You can't help," came Fox's voice from the tree, "because YOU JUST DON'T FIT IN!"

"YES I DO!" cried
Moose, charging at the tree.

CRASH! SMASH!

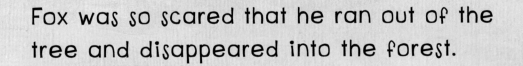

Fox was so scared that he ran out of the
tree and disappeared into the forest.

The fairies were shaken and
scared, but not hurt.
"Thank you, Moose!" they said.

"You saved us, even though
we were mean to you!"
cried Mouse.

"Of course," said Moose,
"I took the Fairy oath.

Fairies are kind to all creatures,
Fairies are not mean or bitter,
Fairies help others in trouble or need..."

"And make pretty pictures with glitter!"
everyone joined in.

"We were just about to make some glitter pictures! Will you join us?" asked Miss Twinkle.

"But you said I don't fit in," said Moose, sadly.

"We were wrong!"
cried the fairies,

"you are the best
fairy of all!"

"That's right!" said Miss Twinkle.
"In fact, you don't just 'fit in'...

...YOU BELONG!"

And for the first time in a very long time,
Moose felt that he really did.